Also by Alan MacDonald

Ask Oscar

Oscar and the Dognappers

OSCAR
AND THE
CATASTROPHE

ALAN MACDONALD

ILLUSTRATED BY SARAH HORNE

EGMONT

For Jack Jenkinson, who has already written a book
AM

For Harry and Thomas H
SH

EGMONT
We bring stories to life

First published in Great Britain 2018
by Egmont UK Limited
The Yellow Building, 1 Nicholas Road, London W11 4AN

Text copyright © 2018 Alan MacDonald
Illustrations copyright © 2018 Sarah Horne

The moral rights of the author and illustrators have been asserted

ISBN 978 1 4052 8724 1

67272/1

A CIP catalogue record for this title is available from the British Library

Typeset by Avon DataSet Ltd, Bidford on Avon, Warwickshire
Printed and bound in Great Britain by the CPI Group

CONTENTS

CHAPTER 1

MOVING IN

On the first floor of 18 Beach Road a boy and his dog stood looking out of a window. The boy was wearing blue patterned pyjamas while the dog wasn't wearing anything, apart from a collar and a worried frown. The dog's name was Oscar and his boy was called Sam. Anyone passing by on the road wouldn't have suspected there was anything out of the ordinary about them.

'It's okay, Oscar, it's only a furniture van,' said Sam. 'I think someone's moving in next door.'

Oscar pressed his nose closer to the window.

He didn't trust vans, not since a black one had carried off two of his friends and they'd had to rescue them from a dog pound. This van, however, was large and blue with *Heaver and Sons Removals* written on the side. It was parked outside number 20, the house next door that had a *SOLD* sign in the front garden. The workmen were unloading the furniture onto the pavement.

'Look, there's a pet basket,' said Sam. 'You never know, they might have a dog.'

Oscar gave him a look as if to say there was only one dog in the neighbourhood and that was him.

Downstairs a heady smell of coffee, toast and sausages filled the kitchen as Mr Shilling made breakfast. The coffee was for him, the toast for everyone, and the sausages were for Oscar, who claimed tinned dog food was not fit to eat.

'It looks like someone's moving in next door,' said Sam, pouring himself some cereal.

Dad nodded. 'Yes, I saw the van,' he said, closing the kitchen door. He lowered his voice. 'Before your mum gets down, you haven't forgotten, have you?'

'Forgotten what?' asked Sam.

'Her birthday of course – it's next Saturday. I wrote it on the calendar so you wouldn't forget.'

Sam *had* forgotten. He rarely looked at the calendar because most of the time it recorded things like 'dentist appointment' or 'parents evening'. Saturday still gave him a week to get a present but he had no idea what to get. As it was almost the end of the summer holidays, he'd spent most of his pocket money too.

'What are you giving her?' he asked.

'Me? I'm working on a little idea,' said Dad. 'I'll show you when it's ready.'

Sam nodded. He hoped it wasn't one of his dad's less successful inventions like the Hercules Speedy Pop-up Toaster, which had almost set fire to the kitchen.

Dad set Oscar's food bowl down on the floor. 'There's a birthday list on the fridge,' he said.

Sam read the list, which he obviously hadn't noticed.

A holiday – anywhere hot
A new car!
Swimming costume
Beach towel
Slippers

4

He was pretty sure he couldn't afford a holiday, unless his mum wanted a bus ride to Winklesea. They hadn't gone away this summer because his parents had been busy running the beach cafe, which Dad had bought after selling one of his inventions. Originally it was called The Toast Cafe, but then Sam and Oscar had the genius idea of turning it into The Waggy Dog Cafe – the only cafe in Little Bunting to welcome dogs.

Oscar barked loudly, interrupting his thoughts. Usually this meant someone was coming and a few seconds later the doorbell rang.

It was Mr Trusscot, their busybody neighbour, who was known in Sam's family as Mr Fusspot. As leader of the town council, Trusscot had once tried to turn most of the town into a dog-free zone, so he and Oscar were old enemies.

'Mr Trusscot, how nice to see you,' lied Dad.

Trusscot nodded to them. As usual, he was wearing his brown tweedy suit with a checked bow tie. Sam thought he'd probably been born wearing a suit. Oscar eyed him suspiciously.

'I imagine you've heard the news,' said Trusscot. 'We're getting a new neighbour.'

'So I gather,' said Dad. 'I expect you're going to tell me who it is.'

'As a matter of fact I can,' replied Trusscot, smugly. 'It's Mrs Bentley-Wallop.'

'Mrs *WALLOP?*' giggled Sam.

'*Bentley*-Wallop,' said Mr Trusscot. 'And I fail to see what's funny about it. Perhaps you've heard the name?'

'I haven't,' replied Dad. 'I think I'd remember a name like that.'

'Well from what I hear she's from a wealthy family and she's very well connected,' said

Trusscot. 'She's just the sort of person we need to improve this neighbourhood.'

Sam and Dad exchanged looks. Mr Trusscot was always talking about improving the neighbourhood. He complained that the Shillings' doorbell played 'Jingle Bells' and their garden was a disgrace, littered with batteries and bike parts for Mr Shilling's inventions.

'In any case, she's arriving this morning so you might want to tidy up,' said Trusscot.

'Why? Is there going to be an inspection?' asked Dad.

'I suppose that's one of your jokes,' said Mr Trusscot, frostily. 'I'm sure we all want to make a good impression on Mrs Bentley-Wallop. I for one am very much looking forward to meeting her.'

'Good, then I won't keep you,' said Dad.

'Oh, and one more thing,' said Trusscot. 'You'd better keep your filthy dog away from her.'

Oscar bristled.

'He's not filthy,' said Sam, crossly. 'He had a bath last week and, anyway, he wouldn't hurt a fly.'

'Well I don't want him upsetting Mrs Bentley-Wallop,' said Trusscot. 'My advice is to keep him indoors where he can't do any harm.'

Oscar took a step forward and proceeded to give Mr Trusscot's hand a thorough licking. He knew very well this would annoy him. Trusscot hated dogs and he didn't want any of their slobbery germs. He pulled his hand away.

'He's only trying to be friendly,' said Sam.

'Well I'd rather he didn't,' snapped Trusscot, wiping his hand on a hanky.

'Anyway, thank you for calling by and if we ever need your advice we'll be sure to ask,' said Dad. He closed the door and rolled his eyes at Sam.

'Nincompoop!' he said and marched back to the kitchen.

Sam waited till he was gone and looked at Oscar.

'Uh oh.'

'If he thinks I'm staying indoors to please him, he can forget it!' said Oscar.

'It's only old Fusspants, ignore him,' said Sam. 'Anyway maybe Mrs Thingy Wallop *likes* dogs.'

'Who doesn't?' asked Oscar.

'Mr Fusspot for one,' said Sam. 'But I saw a pet basket, so maybe she's got a dog herself. We should go next door and find out.'

'All right, as long as it's not a poodle,' said Oscar. 'They never stop yapping.'

Sam looked round as his Dad reappeared, heading upstairs.

'Who are you talking to?' he asked.

'No one,' said Sam. 'Just, you know – Oscar.'

Dad sighed and shook his head.

'How many times? He's a dog, Sam. He doesn't understand a word you're saying!'

CHAPTER 2

UPPITY

Sam had first discovered that Oscar could speak the day after he'd arrived on a number 9 bus. His very first words were: 'I'm not an idiot, you know.' Actually, those were his second words because on the first evening he'd murmured 'Goodnight,' just as Sam was about to go to sleep. Sam hadn't believed his ears that time, but by now he was used to the fact that Oscar could hold a conversation. It was a secret known only to the two of them. Sam hadn't told his parents or even his best friend Louie, although sometimes he wondered if Louie suspected.

Next door the removal men trooped in and out as the morning wore on, carrying carpets and items of furniture. Sam saw white rugs, table lamps and even a couple of statues that had forgotten to get dressed.

Eventually a car drew up and Mrs Bentley-Wallop herself got out. Sam had to admit she was more interesting than Mr Trusscot who was about as glamorous as a cardigan. Mrs Bentley-Wallop had thick blonde curls, bright red lipstick and a double chin. She wore a long, grey, fur-trimmed coat. Sam thought she looked like a film star – although obviously quite an old one.

Back inside, he told his mum about their new neighbour.

'Bigley-Wallop? Are you sure that's her

name?' asked Mum.

'Bigley or Bottomly, I don't remember,' said Sam. 'But Mr Trusscot says we ought to keep Oscar indoors so we don't upset her.'

'Mr Trusscot can mind his own business,' said Mum. 'All the same we ought to make Mrs Whats-her-name welcome. Maybe I'll pop round later to say hello.'

'I'll come!' said Sam, eagerly. He'd never actually been next door. He wanted to know what the naked statues were for. Besides, he was keen to find out if their new neighbour had a dog. That would be the final straw for Mr Trusscot – two dogs on the road in barking distance of each other. He might even have to move to Australia.

After lunch they called next door. Mum took

a tin of her homemade flapjack. Oscar came along but at the gate he stopped and hung back, leaving Mum to go ahead.

'What's wrong?' asked Sam.

'There's a funny smell,' said Oscar, wrinkling his nose.

Sam sniffed. 'I can't smell anything.'

'Your nose doesn't work,' said Oscar. 'I know that smell and it means trouble.'

It was too late to go back now. Mum had rung the bell and Mrs Bentley-Wallop was opening the door. Sam hurried to join them. Their new neighbour wore quite a lot of make-up but that wasn't what caught Sam's attention – it was the enormous white cat sitting in her arms. It was as big as a pumpkin with green eyes that glittered when it saw Oscar.

'We live next door,' said Mum. 'We brought

you a little welcome present.'

'Oh, how terribly kind of you!' cried Mrs Bentley-Wallop in a plummy voice. 'Flapjack! I haven't eaten that in years!'

'Mum made it. Her flapjack's the best,' Sam informed her.

'I'm sure it tastes delicious!' said their neighbour. Her face fell when she spotted Oscar. 'Oh goodness, you have a dog!'

'Yes, this is Oscar,' Sam told her.

'Doesn't he have a lead?' asked Mrs Bentley-Wallop.

'He doesn't need one, he's very well behaved,' said Sam. He shot Oscar a warning look.

'Of course, I'm a cat-lover myself,' Mrs Bentley-Wallop was saying. 'This is Carmen, isn't she a darling pusskins?'

The big cat purred as Mrs Bentley-Wallop

stroked her head. She narrowed her eyes at Oscar whose ears twitched. Plainly he didn't think Carmen was a darling pusskins at all.

'I'd *love* to ask you in, but as you can see the place is such a state,' trilled Mrs Bentley-Wallop. 'And I'm afraid I don't have dogs in the house. Carmen doesn't like it and they do

make a mess.'

'Oscar isn't messy,' said Sam.

'Well, only a little,' laughed Mum. 'But he is quite clever, sometimes we wonder if he understands what we're saying.'

'Heavens! I hope not!' laughed Mrs Bentley-Wallop.

Carmen wriggled in her arms and she set her down on the floor.

'It's all right, princess,' she cooed. 'No one's going to hurt you. Carmen's a Persian, they're *terribly* sensitive.'

Sam didn't think Carmen looked sensitive. If anything she seemed to be enjoying the fact that Oscar couldn't get at her. She hid behind her owner's legs and peeped out now and then, playing a game of peek-a-boo.

'I'm sure Oscar wouldn't hurt her,' said Mum.

'Perhaps they'll be friends?'

Carmen dared to venture a little closer. She rubbed her back against her owner's legs, purring loudly and swishing her long tail. It was almost as if she was daring Oscar to come after her.

Oscar had seen enough. He barked.

'OSCAR!' cried Mum.

Mrs Bentley-Wallop scooped up Carmen in her arms and stepped back from the door.

'Well, perhaps I ought to get on,' she sighed. 'It was so sweet of you to pop round. I'm sure we'll bump into each other again.'

'Yes, of course . . .' began Mum – but the door had already closed.

They walked back down the path.

'Well that didn't go very well,' said Mum.

'I know,' said Sam. 'I'm not sure she even likes flapjack. And she called Oscar messy!'

'We should never have taken him,' said Mum.

'It wasn't his fault!' protested Sam. 'Carmen was showing off the whole time.'

'She's obviously nervous around dogs,' said Mum. 'You'd better keep Oscar away from her or there's going to be trouble.'

Oscar waited until Mum had gone inside and the door had closed.

'I warned you,' he said. 'I knew I smelled a cat, the worst kind too.'

'What's the worst kind?' asked Sam.

'The uppity kind,' replied Oscar.

Sam had never thought of cats as uppity,

although it was true you couldn't tell a cat what to do. Most dogs would happily fetch a stick if you threw one. A cat would just stare at you as if you'd lost your mind.

'Is she going to stay long?' asked Oscar.

'Probably,' said Sam. 'But there's nothing we can do about it. Anyway, what's so terrible about cats?'

'If you're asking that, you don't know many cats,' replied Oscar, darkly.

'Well you heard Mum, you'll just have to behave or you'll get us into trouble,' warned Sam.

Oscar gave him a look.

'I'm a dog,' he said. 'And dogs chase cats – if we didn't they'd get too uppity.'

CHAPTER 3

WALL GAMES

Over the next few days the Shillings' new neighbour settled in at Number 20. Mr Trusscot wasted no time in calling round with a large bunch of flowers. Unlike Sam and his mum, he was invited in and stayed for half an hour.

The two naked statues eventually appeared in the garden. They were a pair of plump angels, one holding a harp and the other a little bow and arrow. From Sam's house you got a good view of their backs and bare bottoms. He wondered what else Mrs Bentley-Wallop had planned for her garden – maybe a fountain or a boating lake?

However it was Carmen who was Sam's greatest concern. The big white cat appeared every morning and took a leisurely tour of her kingdom. Once she'd seen off any sparrows, she hopped up onto the wall and settled in her favourite spot overlooking the Shillings' garden. Her long white tail swished back and forth like a fan. This routine drove Oscar crazy. Carmen was sitting on 'his' wall where she was maddeningly just out of reach. To make matters worse, he was forbidden to bark or chase her off.

'She's doing it deliberately,' he grumbled.

'Take no notice,' Sam advised. 'She's only doing it to annoy you. Just ignore her.'

But Oscar couldn't ignore it. Up until now this part of Beach Road had been his private territory. Other dogs were welcome to visit but he wasn't sharing it with some snooty-nosed cat.

Matters came to a head on the Tuesday after Mrs Bentley-Wallop arrived. Sam was keeping one eye on Oscar through the kitchen window when Carmen made her entrance. She hopped up onto the garden wall and padded along it, paying Oscar no attention. Oscar sat up. His eyes followed the cat, watching her every move.

'Sam, have you seen my ruby ring anywhere?' asked Mum.

'Er, what?' asked Sam, not really listening.

'I'm sure I left it in the bathroom last night, but now it's vanished,' said Mum. 'You're absolutely sure you haven't seen it?'

Sam looked round. 'I don't even know what it looks like,' he said.

'It's gold with a small red stone,' explained Mum. 'Are you listening to me, Sam?'

Out in the garden, Carmen did something she hadn't done before. She suddenly sprang onto the roof of the Shillings' shed. Oscar barked. This was going too far. The shed belonged to him, or at least to Mr Shilling, who used it as his workshop.

'Sorry,' said Sam, jumping up. 'I just need to check on Oscar a minute.'

By the time he got outside, things were getting out of hand. Oscar was barking excitedly. Carmen sat on the shed roof with her back to him, dangling her tail and swishing it back and forth. Oscar jumped up but the roof was too high to reach. Carmen gave him a pitying look and began to wash her paws. She was clearly enjoying the situation.

'Oscar! Come away,' cried Sam.

But Oscar had other ideas. He suddenly leapt onto the compost bin and from there managed to scramble onto the shed roof. Sam had no idea he could do that.

Carmen backed away up the sloping roof.

Now the tables had turned and Oscar had her trapped. He stood his ground, waiting to see what she would do. Carmen had reached the top of the roof and had nowhere to go.

Suddenly she did something unexpected. She sprang high over Oscar's head and landed on his back, digging in her claws. Oscar yelped in pain as she jumped off. In one great leap she made it back over the wall and into her own garden. Sam thought that was the end of the matter, but Oscar wasn't finished. No mean-eyed moggy was using him as a trampoline and getting away with it.

Sam ran to the wall, just in time to see Oscar land on Mrs Bentley-Wallop's lawn. Then the chase was on. A white ball of fur flew past with Oscar close behind. The two of them whizzed round the garden using the statues as a roundabout. They shot under a garden bench and trampled through a bed of purple lavender.

Finally, Carmen decided to make a stand. She hopped up onto a block, which supported one of the two statues. Sam didn't like the way this was going.

'OSCAR!' he cried.

But Oscar pretended not to hear. As Carmen yowled and darted away, he made a flying leap after her. Sam saw the statue wobble like a tower of jelly, then it toppled over and hit the ground.

He buried his face in his hands. The statue lay on its front with its bottom sticking in the air. Luckily, its arms and legs were still attached. The head, however, had rolled across the lawn where it was smiling up at the sky. Oscar trotted over and prodded it with his paw.

Sam felt a wave of panic. Oscar needed to get out of the garden before anyone saw him.

There was no sign of Carmen, who'd vanished from the scene of the crime. Sam wondered if there was time to climb over and drag the statue back onto its stand. But even if he succeeded, it would be pretty obvious it was missing a head. Maybe he could stick it back on with superglue?

'OSCAR!' he hissed as loudly as he dared. Oscar looked round. But before he could move a door banged open and footsteps crunched on the gravel. Mrs Bentley-Wallop stormed into view with a shoe in one hand. Sam ducked below the wall, out of sight.

'Out of my garden, you horrible beast!' roared Mrs Bentley-Wallop, sounding far less plummy and polite.

A high-heeled shoe flew over the wall and landed in a bush. Sam heard Oscar bark and race away. A minute later he trotted back in through the front gate, looking pleased with his morning's work.

For the rest of the day, Sam decided to keep well out of his parents' way. He called for Louie and they took Oscar to the park to play football. He didn't know how much Mrs Bentley-Wallop had seen but she was bound to make a complaint.

When they finally returned late that afternoon Sam's worst fears were confirmed. Through the window, he could see his mum and dad talking to someone. But it wasn't their next-door neighbour. It was Sergeant Wilkins from the police station. Sam knew he should have come clean about the broken statue, but he never imagined that Mrs Bentley-Wallop would call the police!

He trailed into the lounge with Oscar at his heels. Dad looked up. 'Ah Sam, you know Sergeant Wilkins, don't you?' he said.

Sam hung his head. 'It was an accident,' he said. 'He didn't mean it.'

'Who?' frowned Mum. 'The sergeant's been telling us about a burglary.'

Sam stared. 'A burglary? But I thought . . . never mind,' he mumbled.

So the police weren't here about Oscar at all! Maybe Mrs Bentley-Wallop hadn't even noticed that one of her statues was missing a head?

'Anyway, if you think of anything get in touch,' the sergeant was saying. 'I just thought I'd better warn you.'

From what Sam gathered, a house on Hillcroft Drive had been burgled last night. Only one thing had been taken – a gold necklace with a teardrop diamond. Stranger still, the police hadn't found any damage or signs of a break in.

'It's certainly an odd one,' said Sergeant Wilkins. 'But don't you worry, we'll get to the bottom of it.'

'Didn't you say you'd lost a ring?' Sam reminded his mum.

'Yes, but I'm sure it's nothing to worry about. It'll turn up soon,' said Mum.

'Well, if it doesn't, let me know,' said the sergeant.

Sam could hardly take it in. Little Bunting wasn't the kind of place where robberies usually took place – unless you counted seagulls pinching ice-creams out of peoples' hands.

'Anyway, thanks for the tea, Mrs Shilling,' said Sergeant Wilkins, getting to his feet. He headed into the hall with the rest of them following.

'Oh yes, I knew there was something else,' he said, turning round. 'We had a complaint from your neighbour.'

Sam's heart sunk.

'Not Fusspot again!' groaned Dad.

'No, a Mrs Beastly-Wallop,' said the sergeant, squinting at his own handwriting. 'Trespassing in her garden, she says.'

'Sam!' cried Mum.

Sam stared at the hall carpet. He caught sight of Oscar's head poking round the lounge door.

'Actually it wasn't Sam, it was Oscar,' said Sergeant Wilkins. 'I'm told he's been terrorising your neighbour's cat. He broke a statue, too.'

'Only the head!' protested Sam.

Mum and Dad both stared at him.

'So you *do* know about this,' cried Mum. 'Why on earth didn't you tell us?'

'I was going to,' sighed Sam. 'But it wasn't Oscar's fault. Carmen started it, she was on the shed roof . . .'

'Nevertheless, I'm afraid you'll have to pay for the damage,' said the sergeant. 'Your neighbour's not very happy. If I were you I'd keep Oscar out of her garden in future.'

The front door closed at last and Sam was left to face his parents.

'Honestly Sam!' groaned Mum, shaking her head. 'Why did you let Oscar go next door?'

'I couldn't stop him!' protested Sam. 'Dogs chase cats, they can't help it.'

'Well he'll have to learn to help it,' said Dad, grimly. 'I'm afraid from now on Oscar will just have to be kept on a lead like other dogs.'

'*ON A LEAD?*' cried Sam.

Oscar walked off in disgust, muttering something under his breath. Fortunately no one heard him.

'Sometimes you'd almost swear he understands what we're saying,' said Mum.

CHAPTER 4

DIAMOND AND CARROTS

The next morning, Sam found his parents talking in low voices in the kitchen. It turned out that they'd searched the house from top to bottom, but there was no sign of the missing ring. Dad said they were beginning to think it must have been stolen. Mum was certain that she'd left it on the bathroom shelf that night. None of them had moved it, so where could it have gone?

After breakfast Dad took Sam out to his workshop, saying he had something to show him. They talked about the missing ring for a while then he brought out a brightly coloured towel.

'What do you think?' he asked. 'It's Mum's birthday present. I told you I was working on something.'

'Great,' said Sam. 'She wanted a beach towel.'

'Ah but wait till you see this,' said Dad. He pressed a button and to Sam's surprise the beach towel began to inflate. It kept growing and swelling until Sam realised what it was.

'An air-bed!' he said. 'That's amazing . . .'
'I know,' said Dad. 'You can dry yourself or float on it like a lilo. I call it the Towello – a towel and a lilo in one.'

Meanwhile the Towello was still inflating. It grew bigger and bigger, taking up most of the shed until finally . . . BANG!

It burst.

Dad brushed bits of towel and plastic off his clothes.

'Hmm. Oh well,' he said. 'Perhaps I'll give her something else.'

Sam wasn't so sure his mum needed a self-inflating beach towel anyway, but he had problems of his own. He hadn't found a present yet and time was running out.

'Dad,' he said. 'Where could I buy a ring?'

'A ring? You'd have to try a jewellers,' replied Dad. 'But I'm afraid rings are a little expensive.'

'I know,' said Sam, 'but mum's lost hers hasn't she?'

'Ah I see,' said Dad, pushing back his hair. 'The thing is Sam, that ring belonged to your grandma, so it's not really something you can replace.'

'Oh,' said Sam. 'Not even if I found one exactly the same?'

'It's a nice thought,' said Dad. 'But why

don't you buy her something easier – slippers for instance.'

Sam nodded. The truth was he really wanted to get his mum something special for her birthday and he'd bought her slippers the year before. Maybe he'd just take a look around town to see if anything caught his eye? He could take Oscar with him and call for Louie too. He was dying to tell him about the police and the burglary.

Back in the house, Dad reminded him that Oscar had to wear a lead if he was going out. The one in the cupboard had never been used since Sam knew that Oscar hated it. But after the statue incident they didn't have much choice.

Sam held onto Oscar while Dad fitted the lead to his collar.

'There,' he said at last. 'That should do it.'

Oscar glared at the lead as if it was a ball and chain.

Soon they headed off down the road with Oscar tugging like mad. He made a great show of how uncomfortable it was.

'It's not that bad, Oscar,' sighed Sam. 'Other dogs wear them all the time.'

'I am not other dogs,' replied Oscar. 'And how would you like to be dragged along like a shopping trolley?'

Sam sighed. If anyone was getting dragged along, it was him. Every time Oscar ran off to sniff at a tree or a lamppost, the lead went taut, yanking Sam backwards.

They called at Louie's house.

'What's with the dog lead?' he asked, as they set off for the shops.

'Dad says Oscar has to wear one,' explained Sam. 'It's a long story.'

Louie listened wide-eyed as Sam told him about their new neighbour, Carmen and the statue.

'And that's not all,' he added. 'My mum's ring's gone missing and it might have been stolen.'

'You're kidding!' said Louie. 'A burglar actually broke into your house?'

Sam shrugged. 'We don't know but that's what my Dad thinks.'

Louie looked impressed.

'I didn't know your Mum *had* a diamond ring,' he said.

'She doesn't, it was a ruby or something,' said Sam. 'It belonged to my Grandma.'

'You know what we ought to do?' said Louie. 'Next time we should set a trap. We could fill a bucket and balance it on top of your door. When the burglar walks in they get covered in super glue and they won't be able to move.'

'Good idea,' laughed Sam. 'But my Dad says he's working on a burglar alarm.'

All the same he was glad that Oscar slept on his bed. If they had been burgled, it was strange that Oscar hadn't heard anything. Usually he barked like crazy before the postman even reached the door.

They'd reached the high street where Jarman's the Jewellers stood on the corner. Sam didn't often go shopping and he'd certainly never set foot inside a jewellery shop. He peered at the window display where diamonds, emeralds and sapphires sparkled under tiny spotlights. The prices had a lot of noughts in them and were about a thousand times more than he could afford.

'Perhaps this wasn't such a great idea,' he sighed.

'Why not? I thought you wanted to buy a ring?' said Louie.

'I do, but not for a thousand pounds!'

'That's just the stuff they put in the window,' argued Louie. 'We might as well take a look now we're here.'

The door announced them with a loud clang. Sam took a deep breath and followed Louie in, tugging Oscar on his lead. Inside the shop, glass cases displayed a bewildering array of bracelets, rings and necklaces. A silver-haired assistant looked up, surprised to see two scruffy schoolboys dragging a dog.

'I'm afraid dogs aren't allowed in the shop,' she said, sharply. 'He'll have to wait outside.'

'It's okay, he won't be any trouble,' replied Louie. 'He'll just sit quietly while we look around.'

The assistant didn't look too happy about it. Sam whispered to Oscar to lie down which he did, eventually. Gold rings and necklaces didn't interest him; if the shop had sold sausages that would have been a different matter.

'How can I help you?' asked the shop assistant.

Sam hesitated. 'Well, um, I was wondering . . .'

'He wants to buy a ring for his mum,' interrupted Louie. 'It's her birthday.'

'How nice,' said the woman. 'Well, as you see, we've plenty of choice. What kind of ring did you have in mind – gold, silver or costume jewellery?'

'Oh it's not for a costume,' said Sam. 'I wanted one like my grandma's – it had a little red stone.'

'You mean a ruby?' asked the assistant.

Sam nodded. He wasn't exactly an expert on jewellery. He noticed Oscar taking an interest in one of the glass cases. The sooner they got out of here the better, he thought. Typically Louie had wandered off to look around instead of watching Oscar.

'Obviously rubies can be quite expensive but it depends on the setting,' the assistant was explaining. 'Some gold rings are nine carat, while others are eighteen or twenty-four carat.'

'Carrot?' said Sam. He thought the shop sold jewellery, not vegetables.

The assistant sighed. 'It's probably best if I show you.'

Sam waited while she reached into the window for a set of rings. All of them looked a million times more expensive than he could afford.

'This one is a ruby set in nine carat gold . . .' began the assistant. But Sam had stopped listening. Across the shop he'd caught sight of Oscar. He was standing on his hind legs,

with his front paws resting on one of the glass
display cases. He pawed at it excitedly as if trying
to reach a juicy bone.

'Good heavens!' gasped the assistant.

'OSCAR!' cried Sam.

The glass case shook under Oscar's weight.
Rings and pairs of earrings started to fall from

their stands like raindrops. Sam panicked. Any minute the whole thing might topple over and shatter into pieces. He rushed over but Louie got there first. He brought Oscar to the ground with a flying rugby tackle.

'It's all right, I've got him!' he panted, as Oscar struggled to escape.

The shop assistant looked like she might have a heart attack. She marched to the door and swung it open.

'OUT! BOTH OF YOU!' she ordered. 'And take your dog with you!'

A moment later they were back on the street.

'Well I won't be going in there again,' grumbled Louie, setting Oscar down on the ground. Sam shook his head.

'That was a disaster,' he said. 'I didn't understand a word she was saying. Why do all the rings have carrots?'

'Maybe in case you're hungry,' suggested Louie. 'But you couldn't afford them anyway. I told you it was a waste of time.'

Sam gave him a withering look. If Louie hadn't insisted he'd never have gone into the shop in the first place.

Oscar had wandered off to stalk some pigeons. Sam hurried over to grab his lead, which was dragging in the dirt. He crouched down with his back to Louie, so they wouldn't be heard.

'What were you playing at?' he whispered. 'I told you to lie down.'

Oscar looked at him.

'I was trying to tell you, it was there right under your nose!' he said.

'What was?'

'Your mum's ring! The shiny gold one!'

Sam groaned. 'Oscar, there are hundreds of gold rings,' he explained. 'It doesn't mean that one was my mum's!'

'Oh,' said Oscar. 'Well you might have told me.'

Louie came over to join them.

'You're doing it again – talking to him like he's a person,' he complained. Sam shrugged.

'Lots of people talk to their dogs,' he said, getting up.

'Not the way you do,' said Louie. 'People will start to think you're mad. Anyway, have we finished shopping or not? I'm bored.'

They walked on. Sam still had to find his mum a present and he was running out of ideas. Eventually he spotted a silver bangle on a market stall and bought it. It had five lucky charms in the shape of stars and moons. It wasn't a ruby ring but it was all he could afford. Louie suggested they take Oscar down to the beach.

'You know what would really make your mum's birthday?' he said, as they turned onto Beach Road.

'What?' asked Sam.

'Finding her ring,' said Louie.

'Well obviously,' agreed Sam. 'It belonged to my grandma so Dad says it can't really be replaced. But I told you, we've looked everywhere.'

'Unless it *was* stolen,' said Louie. 'Then we could find out who took it.'

'Us?'

'Yes, why not? We could be like detectives on TV looking for clues and stuff,' said Louie, warming to the idea. 'I bet we'd be brilliant at it, too. We're both pretty good at puzzles.'

Sam wasn't sure detective work was quite the same thing. It sounded like one of Louie's half-baked ideas, which usually ended in trouble. All the same, he knew that finding the ring would mean a lot to his mum . . . he imagined the look on her face when she unwrapped her present and saw what it was.

Oscar's lead went taut as he nosed in the gutter. A moment later he came trotting back and dropped something at Sam's feet. It was a small, velvet bag, the kind used for keeping jewellery. When Sam looked inside, it was empty. Louie seemed delighted.

'You see!' he cried. 'Oscar's found a clue already! He can be our detective dog!'

CHAPTER 5

STOP THIEF!

Back at Louie's house, the junior detectives settled down with peanut butter sandwiches to go over the evidence. Oscar crunched on a dog biscuit, which Sam had brought with him. They had found a copy of the *Bunting Post*, which carried the story on the front page under the headline:

POLICE BAFFLED BY JEWEL THEFTS!

The report said three houses in the neighbourhood had been burgled, with gold and silver jewellery taken. Inspector Duff said the police were continuing with their enquiries

– which sounded as if they'd asked politely for any robbers to come forward.

Louie finished reading.

'That settles it,' he said, triumphantly. 'Your mum's ring was stolen.'

'You don't know that,' argued Sam.

'Come on,' said Louie. 'Three other houses and they all had jewellery taken, you're not telling me that's a coincidence?'

Sam pulled a face. Louie had a point.

'And there's another thing,' Louie went on. 'The houses were all in the same area, not far from you.'

'What's funny about that?' asked Sam. 'Maybe the burglar's just a bit lazy. What I don't understand is that they only took gold rings and stuff. Why not steal TVs or anything else?'

'Dunno,' replied Louie. 'I guess jewellery fits

in your pocket easier than a TV.'

Oscar squirmed between them and stood on the newspaper. Sam had sometimes wondered whether he could read as well as talk.

'It could be someone we know,' Louie pointed out. 'They're not necessarily going *to look* like a burglar.'

Sam had never thought of this. They decided to draw up a list of suspects, starting with people who had visited Sam's house recently.

SUSPECTS
The postwoman
The window cleaner
Mr Trusscot
Mrs Porter

Sam read through the list again. Most of the

TRUSCOTT

MRS PORTER

THE POSTWOMAN

THE WINDOW CLEANER

SUSPECTS
FOR / AGAINST

suspects seemed as likely as each other. The window cleaner had a ladder, which would come in handy for a burglary, but the postwoman was new so they didn't know whether she could be trusted. Mr Trusscot was always poking his nose into other people's business, while Mrs Porter was about a hundred years old. Sam doubted if she could break into a tin of biscuits, but you never knew.

'It could be anyone,' he sighed hopelessly.

Louie pulled the newspaper out from under Oscar's feet.

'What if they try it again?' he asked.

'Who? The robbers?' said Sam.

'Yes, maybe that's how you catch them,' explained Louie. 'You just have to keep watch to see if they try to rob another house.'

'Yes but which one?' asked Sam. He didn't

see how they could keep watch on every house in the town. All the same he didn't have any better ideas and Louie was keen to get started on their detective work. They agreed to each keep an eye on their own street and then report back later.

That night, Sam stared out of his bedroom window before getting into bed. The street lamps were on and darkness had fallen. A car went past and somewhere in the distance the church clock struck nine.

'See anything?' asked Sam.

'Only a cat,' replied Oscar. 'She's been there for ages.'

Sam spotted the ginger cat on the wall at the end of the garden. He gave up and climbed into bed, turning off the bedside lamp.

'Wait a minute,' said Oscar. 'Who's this?'

Sam slipped out of bed and fumbled around in the dark looking for his dressing gown.

Together they peered down into next-door's garden where the two statues stood like bare-bottomed sentries. Carmen crossed the lawn and stopped to stare at the ginger cat. The two of them slunk out of sight.

'It's only Carmen,' said Sam. 'I'm going back to bed.'

Just then they heard a gate creak. This time Sam thought he did see something: a dark figure creeping down the path. Louie was right – the jewel thief was back and this time he was planning to rob Mrs Bentley-Wallop! Sam thought she was just the kind of person who might have a lot of jewellery in the house.

'Shouldn't we call the police?' he asked.

'No time,' replied Oscar. 'If we wait for them it'll be too late.'

Sam thought that might not be a bad thing, but he followed Oscar onto the landing and crept downstairs. He was pretty sure the police advised you not to tackle burglars by yourself. Oscar didn't listen to advice though; he acted on his own doggy instincts. They opened the back door and went out into the cool night air. Sam shivered and wrapped his dressing gown around him. Nothing stirred except the wind.

'I think he got away,' whispered Sam, hopefully.

But even as he spoke a light came on in Mrs Bentley-Wallop's downstairs window.

'He's in the house,' said Oscar. 'We'll wait here till he comes out.'

'Then what?' asked Sam.

'Then we catch him in the act,' said Oscar.

He made it sound simple, like catching a bus. This was all Louie's idea and he wasn't even here to help, thought Sam. Oscar had already jumped up onto the compost bin and was scrambling onto the wall. Sam sighed heavily and followed.

In next-door's garden they crouched behind the headless stone statue. Sam's heart was racing. The burglar didn't seem to be in any great hurry. At last they saw the downstairs light go off. Sam peered into the darkness, holding his breath. A back door clicked shut and for a second he glimpsed a figure creeping past a window. Their face was hidden by a hood so they looked like a goblin, carrying a sack.

'Here he comes,' said Oscar. 'Leave him to me.'

Sam nodded. He wasn't planning on tackling the burglar himself. Footsteps came towards them on the gravel path. Something jangled,

possibly the bag stuffed with gold and silver jewellery. The thief walked past so close that Sam could hear him humming to himself. Suddenly Oscar sprang out from his hiding place.

'What the devil . . . ?' cried the burglar.

The next moment he was flat out on the grass with Oscar sitting on top of him.

'MMFF! GEROFF!' he shouted, twisting round.

Sam shone the torch on his face. The hood of his coat had fallen down revealing a bald, egg-shaped head.

'MR TRUSSCOT!' gasped Sam.

'Who did you think it was, you blithering halfwit!' cried Trusscot. 'Get your filthy mutt off me!'

Sam pulled Oscar away by his collar.

'But why are you breaking into Mrs Bentley-Wallop's house?' he asked.

'Breaking in? I have a key!' cried Trusscot, jangling a whole bunch of them. 'She asked me to feed her cat and empty the bins while she was away.'

'Oh,' said Sam, seeing the black rubbish bag. 'Sorry.'

Trusscot scrambled to his feet. Sam noticed he had grass stains on his tweedy trousers.

'I've warned you before about that dog,' he grumbled. 'He ought to be locked up!'

'It was a mistake,' said Sam. 'We thought you were the burglar. You won't tell my parents, will you?'

Truscott laughed sarcastically.

'Oh, let's just forget it, shall we?' he said. 'Pretend it never happened?'

'If you wouldn't mind,' pleaded Sam.

'Funnily enough I *do* mind,' snapped Trusscot. 'I mind being knocked down by your dog and sat upon. Believe me, your parents will hear about this and so will the police. Oh yes you wait, young man, you wait!'

He marched off, banging the gate so hard that it almost fell off. Oscar watched him go and wagged his head.

'You must admit, he does *look* like a burglar,' he said.

CHAPTER 6

DANGEROUS DOGS

This time, Sam confessed the whole story to his parents. He had to because they were waiting at the front door when he and Oscar returned. They'd heard raised voices and had come out to investigate.

Back in the kitchen, they listened in stony silence as Sam explained what had happened.

'Why didn't you come and tell us?' asked Mum. 'What if it *had* been a burglar? Who knows what might have happened?'

Sam hung his head. 'Sorry. It wasn't *my* idea,' he mumbled.

'No? Then whose idea was it?' asked Dad.

'Oscar's,' answered Sam truthfully.

Mum and Dad looked at each other in despair.

'Sam, you've got to stop blaming Oscar for things that are your fault,' said Dad. 'He doesn't have ideas - he's just a dog.'

They sent him straight up to bed, saying they'd discuss his behaviour in the morning.

At breakfast Sam's parents took up where they'd left off.

'What were you thinking, sneaking around in the dark?' demanded Dad.

'It was Mr Trusscot who was sneaking around,' said Sam. 'How were we to know it was him?'

Fortunately Oscar interrupted by bringing

over his bowl over and setting it down on the floor. With everyone busy talking; no one had remembered to feed him. Sam went to find him some food as the phone rang in the hall.

As he was filling the bowl, he caught sight of something shiny on the kitchen floor. It was half hidden under Oscar's brown beanbag where he sometimes took a nap. Sam picked it up. It was a tiny pearl earring.

'Look at this!' he said, glad to change the subject.

Mum took it from him and examined it.

'That's odd. It's not one of mine. I've never seen it before,' she frowned. 'Where did you find it?'

'Under Oscar's cushion,' replied Sam. 'But if it's not yours, how did it get there?'

Neither of them knew. Dad came back into

the kitchen, wearing a worried expression.

'That was Sergeant Wilkins on the phone,' he said. 'He'd like us to call in later at the station. Oscar has to come too.'

Around eleven o'clock Sam found himself sitting in the police station beside his mum. Oscar also sat on a chair as the sergeant said the conversation involved him. Sam had never been interviewed by the police before and his stomach was twisted with nerves. To calm himself, he read the notices pinned on the wall. One dog-eared poster was for a wanted criminal. The face looked vaguely familiar, although obviously Sam didn't know any wanted criminals.

Sergeant Wilkins folded his arms. 'I'm sure

you know why you're here,' he began. 'We've had a complaint about Oscar.'

'Sam's told us what happened and he's extremely sorry,' said Mum. 'It won't happen again.'

'Oscar's sorry too. You can't tell but he is,' said Sam.

Oscar wagged his tail, which didn't really help matters much. The sergeant took out a pen.

'That's all very well but I'm afraid Mr Trusscot has made a serious complaint. He claims Oscar attacked him,' he said.

'*Attacked him?*' cried Sam.

The sergeant nodded. 'Well Oscar, have you got anything to say?' he asked.

Oscar had plenty to say but he kept it to himself.

'We all know Mr Trusscot exaggerates,' said Mum. 'He doesn't like dogs either.'

'He hates them!' said Sam. 'Especially Oscar.'

'Talk me through it then,' said the sergeant. 'What exactly happened last night?'

Sam explained how they'd seen a mysterious figure prowling around next door and had gone to investigate.

'Then what?' asked the sergeant.

'Well the burglar was in the house and we saw him leaving,' said Sam. 'That was when Oscar jumped out.'

'He jumped on Mr Trusscot you mean?'

'Yes, but in the dark we thought he was a burglar. He had his hood up,' explained Sam.

'Did Oscar scratch him or bite him?' asked the sergeant.

'No!' answered Sam. 'He just sort of sat on

him like a deckchair. Oscar would never hurt anyone. Look at him!'

They all looked at Oscar who yawned. Sam wished he could at least *try* to help a little.

'It was all just a silly mistake, Sergeant,' said Mum. 'I'll make sure Sam goes round and apologises to Mr Fusspot . . . Trusscot.'

Sergeant Wilkins fiddled with his pen.

'I'm afraid it's not quite that simple,' he said. 'We can't have dogs going round attacking members of the Council.'

'He *didn't attack him!*' groaned Sam. 'And it's the first time he's done anything.'

'The second time,' said Sergeant Wilkins. 'On Tuesday he chased Mrs Bentley-Wallop's cat and broke her statue.'

'Only the head!' said Sam.

'And a few months ago Mr Trusscot

complained that Oscar licked his face,' said the sergeant, checking his notes.

'That's hardly a crime,' said Mum. 'Surely you're not suggesting that Oscar is actually *dangerous*?'

Sergeant Wilkins folded his arms, giving this some thought. Oscar rested his head on Sam's shoulder, looking as dangerous as a feather duster.

'Well, this time we'll let it go,' decided the

sergeant. 'But treat this as a final warning. No more going in other people's gardens or using Mr Trusscot as a deckchair.'

'He won't,' Sam promised.

'Thank you, Sergeant,' sighed Mum, sounding relieved. She got out her purse. 'Before we go, I wanted to give you this. We found it in the house and I thought we'd better hand it in. It's not mine, you see.'

The sergeant stared at the earring, astonished.

'Where exactly did you find this?' he asked.

'Under Oscar's cushion,' said Sam. 'Why?'

'We had several more burglaries last night and Mrs Bentley-Wallop phoned to report a missing earring,' said Sergeant Wilkins. 'A pearl earring just like this one.'

Sam and his mum looked at each other, mystified.

'But that's ridiculous,' said Mum. 'How could one of her earrings end up in my kitchen? She's never set foot in our house.'

'That's a good question,' said the sergeant. 'You say it was hidden under Oscar's cushion?'

Mum nodded.

'Wait, you don't think that *Oscar* took it?' said Sam.

'I don't think anything,' replied the sergeant. 'But we'll keep this as evidence. I'm sure Inspector Duff will be very interested.'

On the way home Sam was careful to keep Oscar on his lead. They didn't need any more trouble. It was bad enough Mr Trusscot claiming that Oscar had attacked him, but now the earring had turned up and made matters worse.

How could it have got there? Sam wondered. Had Oscar gone sleepwalking last night after they'd returned from next-door's garden? If so why would he have brought back a single pearl earring? He'd been known to wear a scarf but this was taking things a bit far!

They turned back onto their road where Oscar immediately started to pull on his lead.

He'd caught sight of the beach where he could run to his heart's content. In any case, thought Sam, the two of them needed to have a serious talk. He promised his mum they'd be back home in half an hour.

CHAPTER 7

COUNTING CATS

Oscar came racing back and shook himself, spraying Sam with wet sand.

'Now what did you want to talk about?' he asked.

'The police,' said Sam. 'Weren't you listening? They think you've got something to do with these robberies.'

'ME?' said Oscar. 'That's barking bonkers!'

'I know, but how do you explain finding Mrs Bentley-Wallop's earring under your cushion?' asked Sam.

'I don't,' replied Oscar. 'Besides I don't wear

an earring. My great-grandfather had one but he was a seadog.'

Sam sighed. Sometimes he couldn't tell whether Oscar was serious or making it up.

'Even so, it doesn't look good,' he said. 'Fusspot's told the police you're dangerous.'

'Huh! That windbag!' snorted Oscar.

'You have to be more careful,' warned Sam. 'Otherwise, well . . .' He trailed off into silence. He knew very well what happened to dangerous dogs. Eventually they had to be put down. But he couldn't bear to say it out loud or even think about it. Besides, he didn't believe Oscar was dangerous or a thief, he was just cleverer than most people – probably cleverer than the police.

Oscar looked up as a seagull wheeled overhead. He was quiet for a moment beating his tail on the sand. Usually this meant he was thinking.

'Here's what we do then,' he said at last. 'It's time we found out who's really behind all these robberies.'

'I thought we'd been trying,' said Sam.

'Trust me, I've got an idea,' replied Oscar. 'We'll need your dad's big gogglers – the ones he uses for bird watching.'

'Big gogglers?' said Sam, blankly. 'Oh, you mean his binoculars?'

'That's the ones. See if you can borrow them tonight,' said Oscar. 'Only it won't be birds we're watching for.'

That evening Sam persuaded his parents to let Louie come for a sleepover. The plan, he explained to Louie, was to keep a round-the-clock watch on the house next door. Sam had no idea what Oscar thought this would achieve, but at least Louie could take a turn in keeping a lookout.

After supper they all trooped up to Sam's bedroom. Louie volunteered to take first watch sitting at the side window. From there they had a good view over next-door's garden.

'What am I looking for?' he asked, focusing the binoculars.

'Anything unusual I suppose,' replied Sam. 'Oscar reckons there's something funny going.'

'Oscar does?' frowned Louie.

'It's hard to explain,' said Sam. 'Sometimes I can sort of guess what he's thinking.'

'Right,' said Louie. 'You do know you're bonkers, don't you?'

For the next hour they took it in turns to keep watch. Dusk fell and one by one the lights came on in the houses along Beach Road. At Mrs Bentley-Wallop's house no one went in or came out, although the lights were on. Sam took second watch but saw nothing but a couple of caravans dawdling past on the road. He lowered the binoculars.

'There's that cat again!' he said.

Oscar trotted over to join him as if this was what he'd been waiting for. The cat wasn't Carmen, it was the ginger one they'd seen hanging around the garden before. It jumped down into a flowerbed and slunk across the lawn. Sam tracked it through his binoculars. Suddenly he spotted a second cat on the roof of the shed. Another one came from the road, sneaking under the gate. Cats were starting to appear from all sides like rabbits on a hillside.

'Take a look at this,' said Sam. 'There's five . . . no six of them.'

'Where are they all coming from?' asked Louie.

The cats were gathering on the lawn. Sam spotted tabby cats, grey cats, lean alley cats and some as black as ink. It was difficult to count but he guessed there had to be a dozen or more. Oscar pressed his nose to the window, watching intently.

'They look like they're waiting for something,' said Louie.

Sam couldn't imagine what. Maybe it was a paws party or a council of cats that met once a year?

'Look, here comes Carmen,' he said.

The big white cat came from the house.

She crossed the lawn to move among her visitors like the Queen.

'This is well weird,' said Louie. 'What are they all doing here?'

Just then a light spilled from a doorway and Mrs Bentley-Wallop appeared, wearing her long, fur-trimmed coat. In her hands she had two bowls, which she set down on the patio. The cats swarmed forward, eager to get at the food. Their host returned with more bowls, then stepped back to watch her visitors feast.

'So that's the big secret?' said Louie, disappointed. 'She's feeding stray cats?'

Oscar shot him a look.

'There must be more to it than that,' said Sam. 'Why wait until it's dark?'

He raised the binoculars again, following Mrs Bentley-Wallop. She was collecting up

the food bowls, even though her guests hadn't finished eating. They crowded around her legs, mewing and complaining. She ignored them and disappeared into the house. On her return she scooped up Carmen and appeared to whisper in her ear. The big white cat seemed to know exactly what to do. She set off, padding down the lawn towards the end of the garden. To Sam's amazement the other cats followed, falling into a ragged group behind her.

'Woah! Where are they going now?' asked Louie.

Sam had no idea but he could guess what Oscar was thinking. There was only one way to find out.

CHAPTER 8

SHORT CUTS

Downstairs, they tiptoed past the lounge where Sam could hear his parents watching TV. They grabbed their coats in the hall. At the back door, Sam hesitated.

'This is crazy!' he whispered. 'We're meant to be in bed.'

'Stay here if you want,' said Louie. 'I want to know where they're going.'

Next door the garden had emptied. There was no sign of Carmen or her green-eyed gang. Sam felt it was probably just as well. Last time he and Oscar had crept out of the house, they'd ended up at the police station. Oscar was padding around the garden, trying to pick up their scent.

'Over there!' cried Louie. Sam caught sight of a dark shadow before it darted away along the wall. He hoped his parents were watching something good on TV. If they went upstairs to check on him there'd be trouble.

The cats were taking a shortcut, following

the long wall along the bottom of the Beach Road gardens. Oscar soon found a way up, and Sam and Louie scrambled after him. The wall was only chest high but Sam had to balance on it like a tightrope walker.

'This better be worth it,' he whispered to Oscar.

The cats seemed to know where they were going and followed Carmen in single file.

Sometimes Sam thought they'd lost them, but then he'd catch sight of a dark shadow as it slipped into the next garden. Staying on the wall required all his concentration. In places it was slippery or overgrown with moss or ivy. Sam almost lost his balance more than once. Added to that, they were crossing gardens that belonged to other people on the road. How were they going to explain it if anyone spotted them?

Sam paused for breath to allow Louie to catch up.

'Where are we?' he asked

'Don't ask me' replied Louie. 'Better keep going or we'll lose them.'

Sam wished Carmen would slow down or take an easier route, such as the street. It was all very well if you were a cat – they could walk along walls in their sleep.

A thick branch barred his path and he pulled it aside, allowing it to spring back after him. A moment later he heard a strangled cry and a rustle of leaves. Turning round, he realised Louie wasn't there.

'Louie!' he called out.

No answer.

'Louie, are you okay?'

'NO!' came the reply. 'I fell off the wall!'

Sam made his way back to the spot. He found Louie lying half submerged in a prickly holly bush, unable to get up. He groaned as if he was dying.

Sam climbed down into the garden to try and help him out.

'What were you doing?' he whispered.

'It wasn't my fault, a branch whacked me in the face!' complained Louie.

oWW!

Sam froze. Further up the garden a light had come on. Whoever lived in the house must have heard something and now they were coming to investigate! Sam ducked down in the bushes, praying that the darkness would hide them.

'SHHH!'

Oscar had come back and was peering down

from the wall. Had Louie heard him speak? Sam put a hand over his friends' mouth just in case.

A door swung open and the owner of the house shuffled out. Sam recognised the elderly man in a dressing gown as Mr Jarvis. He was armed with a milk pan.

'Is someone there?' he asked in a shaky voice.

Sam kept perfectly still, his heart beating like a drum. Mr Jarvis waited a moment and then came further down the garden. If he came much closer he was bound to see them. He'd probably tell their parents. No one was going to believe that they were following a gang of cats.

'Hello? Is someone there?' called Mr Jarvis again. 'Show yourselves or I'll call the police!'

Sam closed his eyes. Maybe they should come out of hiding and try to explain? But before he could move, Oscar took action. He jumped down into the garden and started to bark.

'Oh it's you, is it?' said Mr Jarvis, lowering his milk pan. 'Go on, clear off, you stupid dog!'

Oscar ran off into the bushes. Mr Jarvis shook his head and returned to the house, muttering to himself.

Sam breathed out and helped Louie untangle himself from the holly bush. They slipped out of a back gate and onto the road. Louie was showing off his cuts and scratches when he suddenly remembered something important.

'Oscar spoke!' he cried.

Sam stopped in his tracks. So Louie *had* heard after all. Now they were in trouble.

'You imagined it,' he said.

'No, I heard him! He said, "SHHH!"' maintained Louie.

'That's not a word,' said Sam.

'It is!' argued Louie. 'Anyway, dogs can't say "SHHH!" But Oscar did, I heard him clear as anything.'

Sam looked at Oscar who gave a sort of shrug. There hardly seemed any point in pretending any longer.

Sam sighed. 'I know.'

'*You know?*' repeated Louie. 'You mean you heard him too?'

'Yes,' admitted Sam. 'Look, I couldn't tell you before, but the thing is, Oscar can talk.'

Louie's mouth fell open. Sam could see he wanted to believe it but he was having trouble. Dogs could bark, whine, growl and whimper, but talk – surely that was impossible?

'You mean you've taught him sounds?' he suggested.

'I didn't teach him anything,' replied Sam.

'Right from the first day he could talk.'

Louie laughed. 'This is a joke, right? You're kidding?'

Sam shook his head.

'Okay, make him say something,' said Louie.

Oscar snorted. 'Excuse me, I'm not a performing parrot.'

Louie gaped. 'WOAH!' he cried. 'You actually *can* speak – with like – words!'

'Evidently or you wouldn't understand me,' replied Oscar. 'But you can't tell anyone about this, understand?'

'It's a secret, which is why I couldn't tell you before,' explained Sam. 'I wanted to, but not even my mum and dad know. Oscar thinks it's better that way.'

Louie nodded. He was too amazed and excited to be cross.

'This is brilliant!' he kept saying. 'I knew there was something funny going on. I knew it!'

Sam hoped he could be trusted. One reason he hadn't told Louie was that he sometimes got over-excited. Still, thought Sam, it would be a relief not to have to pretend any longer. At times he'd been bursting to share the secret with someone.

He glanced back along the road, hoping to catch sight of a cat. A lot had happened tonight but it was a pity they'd lost Carmen and her friends. Where were they going and why did they all gather in Mrs Bentley-Wallop's garden? Sam had no answers, or at least none that made any sense. He set off down the road, hoping they didn't run into anyone. Twenty minutes later he was back in his own bedroom, with Oscar fast asleep and Louie still talking.

CHAPTER 9

PAW PRINTS

Friday dawned, the day before Mum's birthday. Sam hadn't even got round to wrapping the silver bangle he'd bought. The truth was he'd been hoping they still might find her missing ring. Oscar claimed they were close to solving the mystery, but Sam didn't see how. All they'd managed to do was follow a bunch of cats and fall off a wall (at least in Louie's case). They'd heard nothing more from the police since they'd visited the station.

Just after ten however, there was ring on the bell. Sam opened the door to see Sergeant

Wilkins and this time he wasn't alone. He introduced Inspector Duff, who he said was in charge of the investigation. Unlike the sergeant she wore a raincoat, although it wasn't actually raining.

'So this is Oscar, is it?' she said once they were settled in the lounge. Oscar glanced up, keeping an eye on the chocolate biscuits on the coffee table.

'Tell me about this pearl earring, the one he hid in his cushion.'

'*Under* his cushion,' said Mum. 'And we don't know Oscar hid it at all.'

'He didn't, I asked him,' said Sam. 'I mean he wouldn't.'

The inspector reached for a biscuit and studied it like a clue.

'Has he ever taken anything before?' she

asked. 'Keys, money – anything like that?'

'No never!' said Sam. 'He took a sausage once but only because it was on the floor.'

The inspector glanced at the sergeant who wrote '*sausage*' in his notebook. She leaned forward, clasping her hands.

'This may sound a little unusual but there's something we'd like to do,' she said. 'Would you mind if we took Oscar's paw prints?'

'Sorry?' said Mum.

'Paw prints – they're like fingerprints only bigger,' explained the sergeant.

Sam and his mum looked baffled.

'Is that really necessary?' asked Mum. 'And anyway, don't all dogs' paw prints look the same?'

'Probably, but it's just for the record,' replied the inspector. 'As a matter of fact we had two more burglaries last night and we found small, muddy prints in one of the houses. I suppose Oscar was at home?'

'He was with me,' said Sam quickly.

This was true, although he didn't mention they were out following cats. He watched as

Oscar gave the sergeant his paw and made an inky paw print on a form.

'Thank you,' said Inspector Duff. 'We won't keep you much longer. There's just one other thing.'

'Don't tell me you want *our* fingerprints too?' said Mum.

Inspector Duff laughed.

'No, that won't be necessary. But if you've no objection we'd like to fit Oscar with one of our pet trackers.'

'A pet tracker? What's that?' asked Sam.

'It helps us keep track of him wherever he goes,' explained the sergeant.

Oscar rolled his eyes and his head sank to the floor.

'You do know he's just a dog?' said Mum.

The inspector smiled. 'I'm sorry but we have

to look into every possibility. Look at it this way, it will help us rule Oscar out of our investigation.'

The tracker device wasn't much bigger than a watch battery and fitted neatly onto Oscar's collar. Sergeant Wilkins explained that it would be possible to track his movements via a mobile phone. Sam thought it was the pottiest idea he'd ever heard. A jewel thief was out there somewhere and the police wanted to check whether Oscar was asleep on his bed.

Later Sam and Oscar went out to the front garden to watch the two policemen depart. Inspector Duff gave them a cheery wave, before they drove off in a police car.

'So she's the one in charge of the investigation?' said Oscar, shaking his head.

'I know,' said Sam.

'And meanwhile I have to wear this ugly *thing* on my collar,' grumbled Oscar. 'If you ask me it's Carmen's paw prints they should be looking at not mine. Have you ever thought *she* could have put that earring under my cushion?'

'Carmen? Why would she do that?' asked Sam.

'To put the police off the scent of course,' said Oscar. 'While they're busy watching me, Carmen can do whatever she likes.'

Sam looked at him.

'Hang on,' he said. 'You're saying *Carmen* is the jewel thief?'

'Not just Carmen, her whole catty gang of friends,' replied Oscar. 'Where do you think they were off to last night?'

'I don't know,' admitted Sam.

'Take it from me, cats are slippery customers,' said Oscar. 'No one pays a cat any attention. They could slip in and out of your house without you even knowing. They take what they came for and then they're gone.'

Sam's mouth hung open. It was hard to believe – a gang of criminal cats making off with people's jewellery? Even if it *were* possible, why would they do it?

'No one would believe us,' said Sam. 'The police will say we're mad.'

'It's no more crazy than suspecting *me*,' Oscar pointed out. 'But you're right about one thing, we'll need proof. That's why we have to catch Carmen in the act.'

'Right,' agreed Sam. 'How do we do that?'

'The same way you catch a fish. We dangle a worm,' said Oscar.

Sam frowned. 'I'm pretty sure cats don't eat worms.'

'Not a real worm,' sighed Oscar. 'I mean we tempt her with something she wants. Now this tracker thing – do you think you can get it off?'

Later that evening, when his parents had gone to bed, Sam helped Oscar to set their trap. They placed the silver bangle on the kitchen windowsill where Carmen was sure to see it. Oscar said it didn't matter that it wasn't real silver, as most cats were too stupid to tell the difference.

Sam had added an extra lucky charm to the bangle which was about the size of a watch battery.

'You think this will work?' he asked.

'Let's hope so,' replied Oscar. 'With cats you can never be sure.'

They hid in the small utility room behind the kitchen with Sam squashed uncomfortably between the washing machine and the boot rack. Oscar lay down on the floor. Now there was nothing to do but wait and watch, hoping that Carmen would turn up.

CHAPTER 10

TWINKLE, TWINKLE LITTLE CAT

Sam woke up to find Oscar's nose in his face. He jolted upright, banging his head against the washing machine.

'SHHH!' warned Oscar. 'She's here.'

It took Sam a moment to remember why he wasn't sleeping in his own bed. He slid over to the door and inched it open a crack to peer out. Oscar's chin rested on his shoulder, breathing heavily. He smelled of sausage meat.

In the hallway stood the big white cat. Sam wondered if she'd got in the way they'd guessed. Carmen turned her head and for a second her green eyes seemed to look straight at Sam. He ducked back behind the door out of sight.

'I don't think she saw me,' he whispered.

Oscar peeped out.

'Keep quiet, let's see what she does,' he said.

They spied on Carmen as she prowled around the kitchen, taking her time. She was obviously used to making herself at home in other people's houses. When she came to

Oscar's bowl she stopped and bent her head to lap at the water. Oscar almost growled and Sam had to hold him back. Carmen certainly had some nerve!

Finally, she ceased prowling and turned her attention to the bangle on the windowsill. Crouching low, she sprang up and landed on the worktop. She looked about her to make sure no one had heard and was coming.

The silver bangle gleamed in the streetlight. Sam leaned forward. If Carmen didn't take it the whole plan collapsed. She sniffed it, and then looked away as if she'd lost interest. Sam hoped she hadn't noticed the extra lucky charm that was different to the others. Carmen bent her head. When she turned round the bangle was in her mouth. She skirted round the sink and jumped down to the floor. They watched her slink out of the kitchen and into the hall, where she disappeared from view.

Sam's hand reached for the door handle.

'Wait, let her go,' warned Oscar.

When they looked again, there was no sign of their visitor. They waited a few seconds more to see if she came back. Finally, Sam slid open the door and they crept out of their hiding place. Carmen wasn't in the lounge or the kitchen. Sam didn't think she could have got in through the letterbox, so that left upstairs. Oscar looked at him and after a moment they crept up.

Carmen wasn't on the landing. The bathroom door was open and Sam went in. The curtains were drifting in the breeze where they'd deliberately left a top window open. Standing on tiptoe, Sam peered out at the starlit sky. He caught sight of the big white cat padding across the rooftops with something in her mouth. Carmen had her prize and now she was heading home.

Back in his room, Sam lay down. He doubted if he'd ever get to sleep with so many thoughts racing round his head. He'd only half believed

Oscar, but now he'd seen it with his own eyes. Carmen was a thief and maybe she wasn't the only one. The only question that remained was *why* would a cat steal jewels?

'Okay I admit it, you were right,' said Sam.

'Of course I was right,' yawned Oscar. 'Like I said, never trust a cat – especially the uppity ones.'

'I still say nobody's going to believe us,' said Sam.

'Then we'll just have to prove it,' said Oscar. 'We can do it tomorrow at your mum's birthday party.'

Sam's eyes blinked open. 'Party?' he said. 'But she's not having a party.'

'Oh didn't I mention it?' mumbled Oscar. 'We'll deliver the invitations in the morning. Get Louie to do it . . .'

His voice trailed off into silence. Sam had no idea what he was talking about. This was the first he'd heard about a party. Who was coming and why? Clearly Oscar had some sort of master plan but it would help if he bothered to explain it.

'Oscar!' whispered Sam. 'Oscar, what do you mean?'

Oscar didn't answer. He was fast asleep, breathing heavily.

CHAPTER 11

THE BOTTOM
OF THE MATTER

Sam glanced anxiously at the clock, wondering if anyone would turn up. On the table sat a small pile of presents and cards that his mum was busy opening.

Dad's present was the most unusual. He'd abandoned the Towello idea. Instead he'd come up with a pair of shoes that had removable tops.

'See, shoes AND sandals!' he said, proudly. 'You can wear either.'

Mum laughed. 'Perfect for when we go on holiday,' she said, kissing him on the cheek.

Sam had drawn his birthday card himself. It had a picture of his family with Oscar sitting in the front.

'I've got you a present, but it's a surprise,' he explained. 'You'll get it later – I hope.'

'Sounds very mysterious,' smiled Mum.

Just then the doorbell rang and Dad went to answer. He returned a moment later with

Sergeant Wilkins and Inspector Duff.

'Oh, hello,' said Mum, a little surprised.

'Happy birthday, Mrs Shilling,' nodded Sergeant Wilkins, removing his hat.

'Many happy returns,' said the Inspector.

'Thank you,' said Mum. 'I'm not sure why you've come but this isn't a good time . . .'

The doorbell rang again. This time it was Louie who'd brought a present, which he'd obviously wrapped himself.

'It's a box of chocolates but I haven't eaten any,' he said proudly, handing it over.

They'd just sat down when the doorbell chimed again. Dad let out a groan. The next arrival was Mrs Bentley-Wallop.

'Is that it? Or is the whole street joining us?' asked Dad.

They weren't, but a few minutes later

Mr Trusscot joined the party. The kitchen was getting overcrowded with not enough chairs to go round.

'I'd better make more coffee,' said Dad. 'And then perhaps someone can tell us what's going on.'

'You tell me,' said Mrs Bentley-Wallop. 'You sent the invitations.'

'Invitations? We didn't send anything,' said Mum.

Oscar trotted over and looked up at Sam. This was his cue and he cleared his throat. He wasn't used to speaking in front of so many people.

'Actually it was our idea, mine and Oscar's' he explained. 'We got Louie to deliver the invitations because we need your help with something. It's a sort of treasure hunt.'

This announcement was greeted with a little grumbling among the guests. Inspector Duff said she was very busy, Mrs Bentley-Wallop claimed to have a hair appointment and Mr Trusscot hated party games of any sort. Nevertheless it was a birthday and now they were here they couldn't very well refuse.

'What's this all about, Sam?' asked Louie as they went outside.

'I'll explain later,' replied Sam. 'It's actually Oscar's idea.'

He hoped Oscar knew what he was doing. If the plan didn't work Sam was going to look pretty stupid. They'd have wasted everybody's time and spoiled Mum's birthday. Worst of all he'd have no present to give her.

Out in the garden, he explained that the treasure they were seeking was a surprise present for his mum. It was probably hidden somewhere close by and Sergeant Wilkins was going to help them find it.

'Me?' said the sergeant. 'What have I got to do with it?'

'You've got that tracker thing on your phone,' said Sam. 'Can you turn it on, please?'

Sergeant Wilkins did as he was asked.

'Is this going to take long?' grumbled Mr Trusscot.

'Yes, I really have to be going,' said Mrs Bentley-Wallop.

Sergeant Wilkins was staring at his phone screen.

'That's odd,' he said. 'It's not picking up Oscar at all, it's showing something else.'

'Great, we can get started then,' said Sam.

They set off with Sergeant Wilkins leading

the way and Oscar trotting eagerly beside him. The tracker device showed the 'treasure' as a red dot on a map. All they had to do was follow the directions to find it. It took them down the garden path, out of the gate and onto the road. Outside number 20 the sergeant halted.

'It's leading us in here,' he said.

'Oh please! This is ridiculous!' spluttered Mrs Bentley-Wallop. 'There's obviously some mistake.'

Inspector Duff opened the gate.

'Let's find out shall we?' she said. 'After you.'

They all trooped in. Instead of taking them to the house, the tracker device led them down the garden. Sergeant Wilkins stopped on the lawn in front of the two naked statues.

'Well this is it,' he said. 'If there is any treasure, it's hidden round here.'

Mrs Bentley-Wallop had suddenly turned pale.

'Right, I think this has gone far enough,' she blustered. 'In fact I'd like you all to leave my garden now or else I'll . . . I'll . . .'

'What? Call the police?' asked Sam.

Inspector Duff folded her arms.

'You seem a little upset, madam, is something the matter?' she asked.

Oscar, meanwhile, had been sniffing around the two naked statues. He circled the one missing a head and began to bark excitedly.

'What is it, Oscar?' asked Sam.

Oscar's answer was to take a few steps back. Suddenly he flew at the statue, launching himself at it like a rocket. For a second the statue wobbled on its stand, then it toppled over with a crash.

Mrs Bentley-Wallop let out a shriek. Sam's mum hid her face. Oscar had really done it this time. The statue had broken clean in two. The lower half was now just a bottom on a chubby pair of legs. Oscar was the only one who seemed pleased, wagging his tail. When Sam went over he couldn't believe his eyes. The statue was hollow as an Easter egg and inside it was filled with glittering jewels.

Sam tipped it up and out tumbled silver necklaces, gold bracelets and diamond rings. Everyone stared in amazement.

'Well I'll be blowed!' said Inspector Duff at last. 'Mrs Bentley-Wallop, perhaps you'd care to explain?'

Mrs Bentley-Wallop opened her mouth but no words came out. She backed away and hitched up her dress. Suddenly she ran across the lawn, tottering in her high heels.

'Stop her!' cried the Inspector.

Sergeant Wilkins gave chase but Oscar was way ahead of him. He raced after Mrs Bentley-Wallop and seized the hem of her dress in his teeth. She stumbled backwards and fell down in a heap. When she sat up, her golden curls sat crookedly on her head. Sergeant Wilkins hauled her to her feet and pulled off the blonde wig.

'Good gravy! You're a man!' gasped Mr Trusscot.

'Well, well, if it isn't Diamond Joe. We've been looking for you,' said Inspector Duff.

'The last we heard you were lying low in London.'

Sam stared. He remembered the poster he'd seen at the police station. He knew he'd seen the face somewhere before. His next-door neighbour was a wanted criminal!

The jewel thief scowled.

'I fancied some sea air, didn't I?' he said, his voice now a growl. 'You'd never have caught me neither, if it weren't for the boy. Him and that nosey dog – too clever by half.'

Oscar sniffed among the pile of jewellery on the grass, looking for something. He prodded it with a paw. Sam bent to pick up and handed it to his mum.

'Happy birthday!' he grinned. 'I got you a bangle too but this is the surprise I told you about.'

Mum stared in disbelief at her ruby ring, the one she thought she'd lost for ever. Kneeling down, she hugged Sam and then Oscar, almost squeezing the life out of them.

'Thank you, both of you,' she sniffed. 'This is the best birthday present ever.'

Diamond Joe was led away in handcuffs to a waiting police car. As he got in, a big white cat appeared on the garden wall. Carmen watched the car speed off down Beach Road and then disappeared into the bushes.

Back at Sam's house, the police had a lot of questions. What made him suspect Mrs Bentley-Wallop and how did he know where the stolen jewels were hidden? Sam explained how they'd set a trap for Carmen by leaving the silver bangle in the kitchen window. She couldn't have known that one of the lucky charms was actually the tracker device from Oscar's collar. Once it was hidden away with the rest of the stolen loot, it led them to the headless statue.

'It was Carmen and her gang who carried out all the burglaries,' explained Sam. 'They'd been trained to sneak in and out of houses through a window or a cat-flap. If they brought back any jewellery they got their reward in cat food.'

'Cat burglars! I'd never have believed it!' said Dad.

'I didn't at first,' admitted Sam. 'It was Oscar who worked it all out. If you ask me, he's the cleverest dog in the world.'

'You can say that again,' grinned Louie.

Oscar wagged his tail and went back to

finishing his breakfast. It was probably true that he was the cleverest dog in the world. Come to think of it, there was no 'probably' about it.